Slippers
at School

by **Andrew Clements**
illustrated by **Janie Bynum**

Dutton Children's Books ● New York

For Matthew and Tricia Clements,
whose love for their dogs has brought joy and inspiration to so many

A.C.

To Mo, who loves her puppies!

XO, J.B.

Text copyright © 2005 by Andrew Clements
Illustrations copyright © 2005 by Janie Bynum

Library of Congress Cataloging-in-Publication Data
Clements, Andrew, date.
Slippers at school/by Andrew Clements; illustrated by Janie Bynum.—1st ed. p. cm.
Summary: Slippers is sad that Laura and Edward have no time for him on the first day of school,
but he finds a comfortable backpack in which to fall asleep before they leave.
ISBN 0-525-47189-8
1. Dogs—Juvenile fiction. [1. Dogs—Fiction. 2. Animals—Infancy—Fiction.
3. Schools—Fiction. 4. Human-animal relationships—Fiction.] I. Bynum, Janie, ill. II. Title.
PZ10.3.C5937Slk 2005
[E]—dc22 2004056181

Published in the United States by Dutton Children's Books,
a division of Penguin Young Readers Group
345 Hudson Street, New York, New York 10014
www.penguin.com/youngreaders

Designed by Beth Herzog

Manufactured in China
First Edition

1 3 5 7 9 10 8 6 4 2

Slippers woke up early one morning.
He walked out of his little house.
He sniffed and listened.

Slippers could hear his family out in the bigger house. It felt like something was going to happen. So Slippers went to wait in the kitchen.

Sometimes Laura would give
Slippers some food.

Not today. Laura was in a hurry.
She was going back to school.

Sometimes Edward would play
pull-the-sock with Slippers.

Not today. Edward had no time to play.
He was helping Laura get ready for school.

Slippers was sad. Laura was going away.
Slippers wanted to go with her.
But school is no place for a puppy.

Laura got her jacket and her backpack from the hall. She was ready to go. Laura called, "Here, Slippers! Come say good-bye!" Edward called, too.

But Slippers did not come.

Mommy said, "The bus is here, Laura."
Daddy said, "We will say good-bye to Slippers
for you." So Laura ran and got on the bus,
and Edward waved good-bye.

It was noisy on the bus. It was a bumpy ride.
But Laura did not care.

She was laughing and talking with her friends.
She was going to school.

At school, Laura found her new room.
Then the teacher showed Laura where to go.

Laura had her own cubby for her jacket
and her backpack.

Laura had her own desk.

And she had a new box of markers.

Laura started to draw a picture.

Over in her cubby, something happened.
Laura's backpack moved.

Out poked a wet black nose,

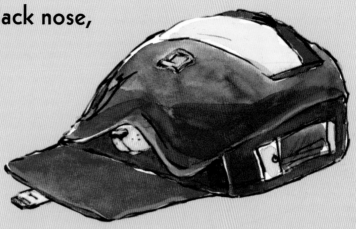

then a pair of shiny eyes,

and then one brown ear,
and then another brown ear.

It was Slippers!

A boy sitting near Laura saw Slippers.
He said, "A dog!"

Laura smiled and held up her picture.
She said, "Yes, this is my dog, Slippers."

The boy said, "No—over there!"
But when Laura turned to look,
there was nothing to see. Slippers was gone.

Slippers smelled something good.
He walked down the hall to the school kitchen.
The cook saw Slippers. She said, "A dog!"

Her helper picked up a hot dog.
He said, "You mean this one?"

The cook said, "No—over there!"
But when the helper turned to look,
there was nothing to see. Slippers was gone.

Slippers trotted into the school gym.
A boy was learning how to jump up and over.

His friend saw Slippers. She said, "It's a dog!"
The boy said, "The teacher called it a horse."

His friend said, "No—over there!"
But when the boy turned to look,
there was nothing to see. Slippers was gone.

Slippers ran down the hall into the office.
The principal saw him and said, "It's a dog!"

The secretary pointed at her sweater.
She said, "This? It's a cat."

The principal said, "No—over there!"
But when the secretary got up to look,
there was nothing to see. Slippers was gone.

Slippers ran around a corner.

Then Slippers stopped and sniffed.
He smelled Laura.

Slippers ran back into Laura's room.
He ran right to Laura's cubby.

LAURA

Slippers wiggled into Laura's backpack.
It was dark and warm inside.
Slippers curled up and went to sleep.

At the end of the day, Laura rode home.
It was noisy on the bus. It was a bumpy ride.

But Laura did not care. She was laughing and
talking with her friends. She was going home.

Mommy and Edward met Laura at the bus. Mommy said, "Come inside and help us look for Slippers. We have not seen him all day."

Laura put away her jacket and her backpack.
Then she started calling.
"Slippers! Here, Slippers!"

And a happy little puppy rushed up to greet her.

Slippers got a big hug from Edward and
Mommy and Laura. Laura said, "School was
fun, Slippers, but I missed you all day."
Edward said, "Me, too!"

Then Laura said, "Could Slippers come
to school someday?"

Mommy said, "It's a nice idea,
but school is no place for a puppy."

And Slippers wagged his tail.